TAMESIDE LIBRARIES

3 8016 01392 6268

TAMESIDE CENTRAL
LIBRARY
TEL: www.
0161-342

WITHDRAWN

D0183157

This book
belongs to:

. . . .

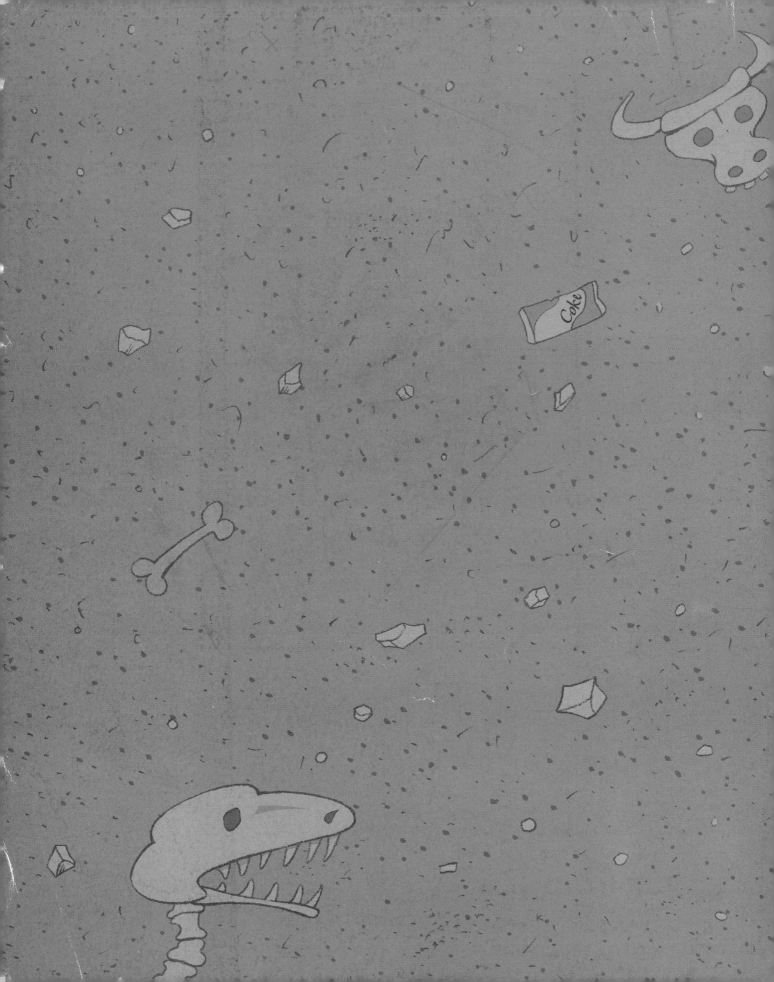

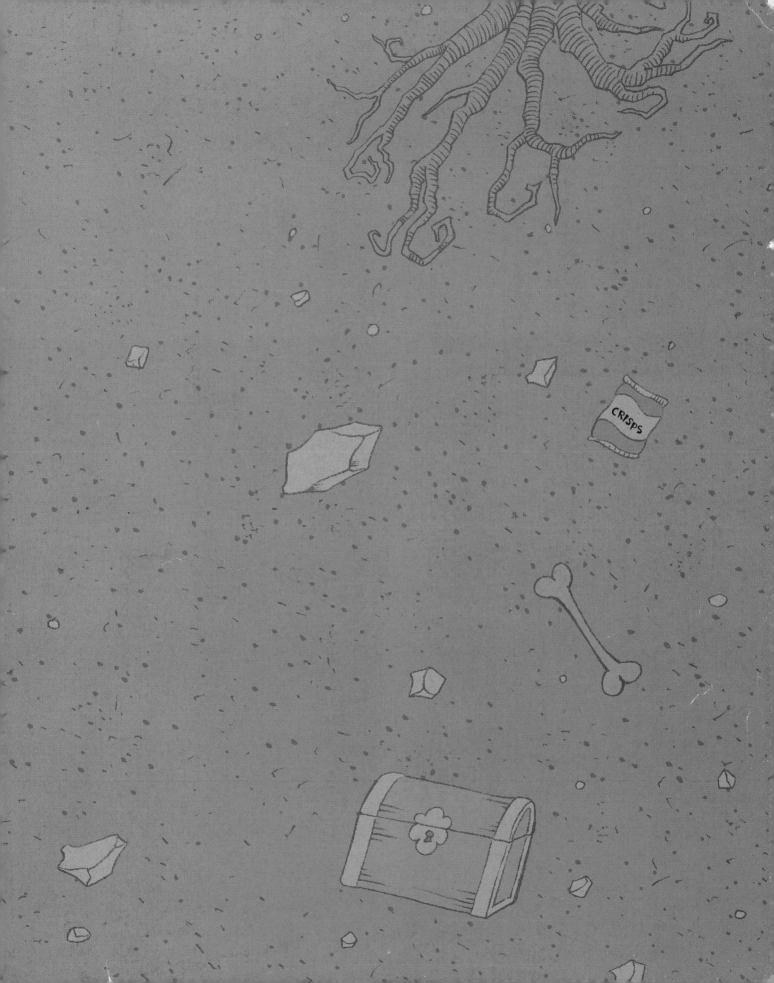

For the Terribly Terrific Amanda

TAMESIDE M.B.C. LIBRARIES	
01392626	
Bertrams	13.03.06
	£4.99

Scholastic Children's Books
Commonwealth House, 1-19 New Oxford Street
London WC1A 1NU, UK
a division of Scholastic Ltd
London ~ New York ~ Toronto ~ Sydney ~ Auckland
Mexico City ~ New Delhi ~ Hong Kong

First published in hardback in the UK by Scholastic Ltd, 2005
First published in paperback in the UK by Scholastic Ltd, 2005

Copyright © Nick Ward, 2005

ISBN 0 439 97367 8

All rights reserved

Printed in Singapore

2 4 6 8 10 9 7 5 3

The right of Nick Ward to be identified as the author and illustrator
of this work has been asserted by him in accordance with the
Copyright, Designs and Patents Act, 1988.

This book is sold subject to the condition that it shall not, by way of trade or
otherwise, be lent, resold, hired out, or otherwise circulated without the
publisher's prior consent in any form of binding or cover other than
that in which it is published and without a similar condition, including
this condition, being imposed upon the subsequent purchaser.

The Terrible Troublesome Troll

NICK WARD

"Time to get up, Billy," called his mum.
Little Billy Goat Gruff sighed. The holidays
were over and it was time to go back to school.
But Billy didn't want to go!

"I've got a tummy ache, Mum," he said.
"You're just hungry," said his mum.

"I've got a sore throat," croaked Billy.
"Not too sore for breakfast," smiled Mum.

"I've got a bad leg!" said Billy, putting on his coat.
"Off you go now, Billy," said his mum, giving him a kiss.
"You know you've
always loved school."

And Billy did love school . . .

. . . it was just getting there that was the problem!

On the way to school Billy had to walk down a long, dark alley. But that didn't scare him.

The lonely mountain path didn't scare him either,
because that's where he met his best friend, Tiny Mole.
But when they reached the rickety-rackety bridge,
Billy and Mole were scared. Because at the rickety-
rackety bridge lived the Terrible, Troublesome . . .

TROLL! Now HE was scary!

"I'm **HUNGRY!**" roared the Troll, stamping his big, hairy foot. He opened Billy's and Mole's school bags and peered inside. "Yum, yum!" he grunted, and down the hatch went their lunch, their lunch boxes, their books and their pencils!

"Now **RUN!**" roared the Terrible, Troublesome Troll, and Little Billy and Tiny Mole ran and ran, over the hill, down the track, all the way to school.

Tiny Mole tapped his tiny foot. "I've had enough of that Terrible, Troublesome Troll," he said. "We need to teach him a lesson."
"But he's too big!" said Billy. "He's too big, he's too bossy and he's too greedy!"

"He's very greedy," smiled Tiny Mole.
And that gave him a brilliant idea...

The very next morning, the two friends met near the rickety-rackety bridge. Little Billy Goat Gruff filled his school bag right up to the top with heavy stones.
"I hope this works," said Billy, as Tiny Mole started to dig a long tunnel. (Moles are very good diggers, you see.)

"Good luck," said Mole. "See you later!"

"Where's Tiny Mole today?" grumbled Troll.
"Oh, he's poorly," smiled Billy.
"But I'm hungry!" shouted Troll, stamping his big, hairy foot. He tipped up Billy's school bag, and down the hatch went Billy's lunch, his lunch box, his books and his pencils and all those heavy stones!

"Lovely!" said Troll.

Every day the two friends
did the same.

Billy filled his
bag with stones;

Mole dug and dug;

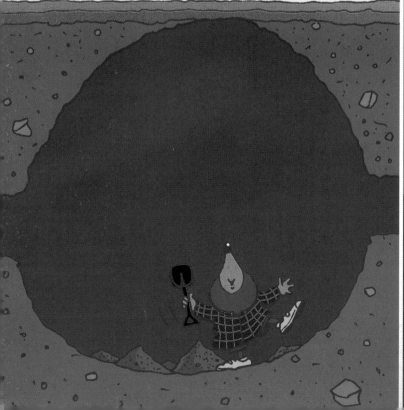

and Troll got
heavier and heavier!

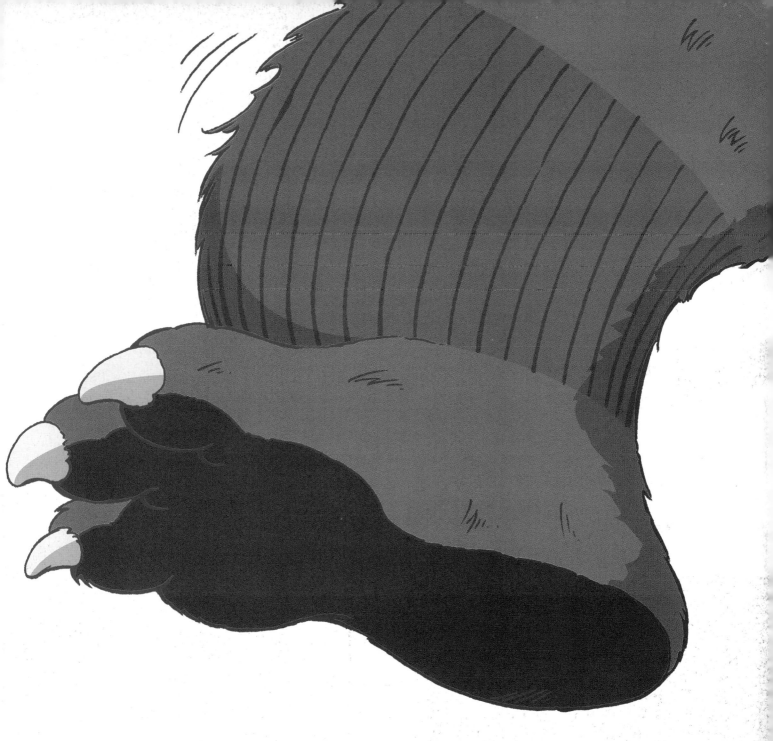

Then, one morning, when Troll stamped his big, hairy foot . . .

CRASH!

He fell through the thin covering of earth and landed in Mole's hole. "That will teach you!" said Tiny Mole.

"I'm sorry," said Troll, as a big tear trickled down his cheek. "I didn't mean to be so terrible and troublesome. Please don't leave me here on my own." And he blubbed and he bawled and he sobbed and he sniffed, until his tears filled the hole right up to his nose.

"Oh dear," said Little Billy, offering him his little handkerchief.
"There, there," said Tiny Mole, "don't cry."
Perhaps the Terrible, Troublesome Troll was really just
a terribly lonely Troll. And THAT gave them another
brilliant idea.

So now, every day, down the long, dark alley, along the lonely mountain path and over the rickety-rackety bridge, Little Billy, Tiny Mole and the not-so-Terrible, Troublesome Troll toddle happily off to school . . . together!

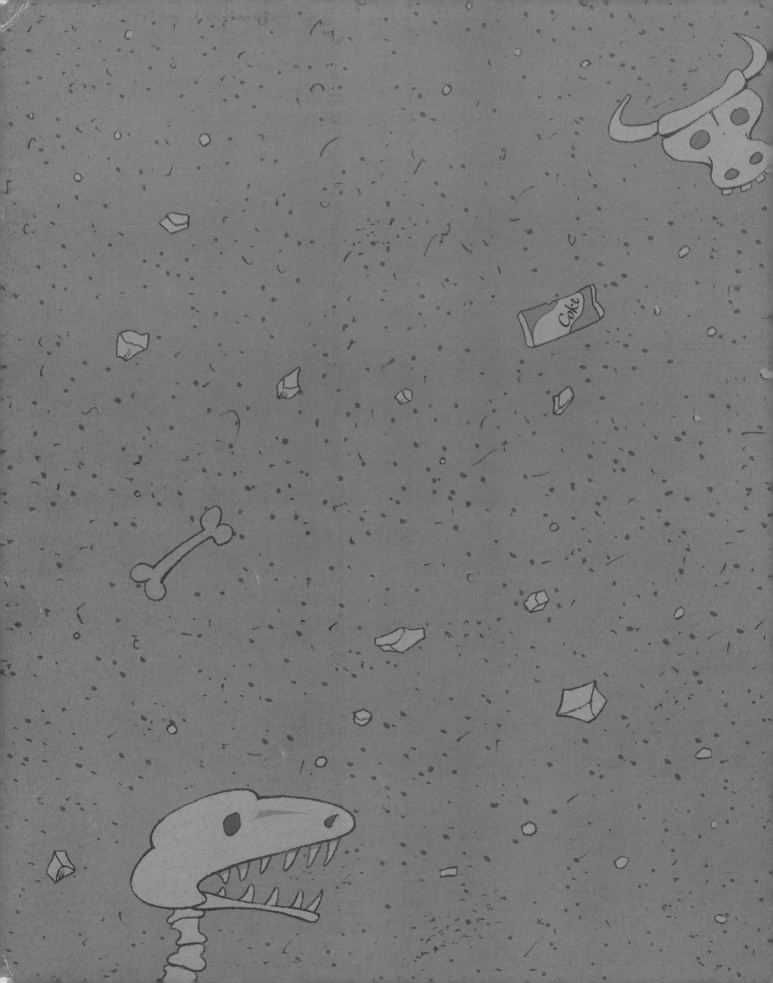